FEED ME!

FEED ME!

Funky Food Science from
Ethan Flask and Professor von Offel

MAD SCIENCE

by Anne Capeci
Creative development by Gordon Korman

SCHOLASTIC INC.

New York   Toronto   London   Auckland   Sydney
Mexico City   New Delhi   Hong Kong   Buenos Aires

No part of this publication may be reproduced in whole or in part, or stored in a retrieval system or transmitted in any form or by any means, electronic, mechanical, photocopying, recording, or otherwise, without written permission of the publisher. For information regarding permission, write to Scholastic Inc., Attention: Permissions Department, 557 Broadway, New York, NY 10012.

ISBN 0-439-20728-2

The Library of Congress Cataloging-in-Publication Data is available.

Copyright © 2000 by The Mad Science Group. All rights reserved.
Published by Scholastic Inc.
Mad Science is a registered trademark of
the Mad Science Group and is used under license by Scholastic Inc.

SCHOLASTIC and associated logos are trademarks and/or
registered trademarks of Scholastic Inc.

12 11 10 9 8 7 6 5 4 3 2 1   3 4 5 6 7 8/0
                                              40
Printed in the U.S.A.

Table of Contents

Prologue

For more than 100 years, the Flasks, the town of Arcana's first family of science, have been methodically, precisely, safely, scientifically inventing all kinds of things.

For more than 100 years, the von Offels, Arcana's first family of sneaks, have been stealing those inventions.

Where the Flasks are brilliant, rational, and reliable, the von Offels are brilliant, reckless, and ruthless. The nearly fabulous Flasks could have earned themselves a major chapter in the history of science — but at every key moment, there always seemed to be a von Offel on the scene to "borrow" a science notebook, beat a Flask to the punch on a patent, or booby-trap an important experiment. Just take a look at the Flask family tree and then at the von Offel clan's tree. Coincidence? Or evidence!

Despite being tricked out of fame and fortune by the awful von Offels, the Flasks doggedly continued their scientific inquiries.

The last of the family line, Ethan Flask, is no exception. An outstanding sixth-grade science teacher, he's also conducting studies into animal intelligence and is competing for the Third Millennium Foundation's prestigious Vanguard Teacher Award. Unfortunately, the person who's evaluating Ethan for the award is none other than Professor John von Offel, a.k.a. the original mad scientist, Johannes von Offel. Von Offel needs a Flask to help him regain the body he lost in an explosive experiment many decades ago. When last seen in *Clue Me In, The Detective Work of Ethan Flask and Professor von Offel*, the professor tried to pin the blame for all the weird happenings at Einstein Elementary School first on Mr. Flask, then on Mr. Klumpp. Too bad the professor was all thumbs! His clumsy attempts really went aground.

Now von Offel is following a whole other tack, inspired by Flask's study unit on food science. After all, if the way to a man's heart is through his stomach, maybe that's the same way the professor can become whole again!

The Nearly Fabulous Flasks

Jedidiah Flask
2nd person to create rubber band

Oliver Flask
Missed appointment to patent new glue because he was mysteriously epoxied to his chair

Augustus Flask
Developed telephone; got a busy signal

Mildred Flask Tachyon
Tranquilizer formula never registered; carriage horses fell asleep en route to patent office

Lane Tachyon
Developed laughing gas; was kept in hysterics while a burglar stole the formula

Percy Flask
Lost notes on cure for common cold in pick-pocketing incident

Archibald Flask
Knocked out cold en route to patent superior baseball bat

Marlow Flask
Runner-up to Adolphus von Offel for Sir Isaac Newton Science Prize

Amaryllis Flask Lepton
Discovered new kind of amoeba; never published findings due to dysentery

Norton Flask
Clubbed with an overcooked meat loaf and robbed of prototype microwave oven

Salome Flask Rhombus
Discovered cloud-salting with dry ice; never made it to patent office due to freak downpour

Constance Rhombus Ampère
Lost Marie Curie award to Beatrice O'Door; voted Miss Congeniality

Roland Flask
His new high-speed engine was believed to have powered the getaway car that stole his prototype

Solomon Ampère
Bionic horse placed in Kentucky Derby after von Offel entry

Margaret Flask Geiger
Name was mysteriously deleted from registration papers for her undetectable correction fluid

Michael Flask
Arrived with gas grill schematic only to find tailgate party outside patent office

Ethan Flask

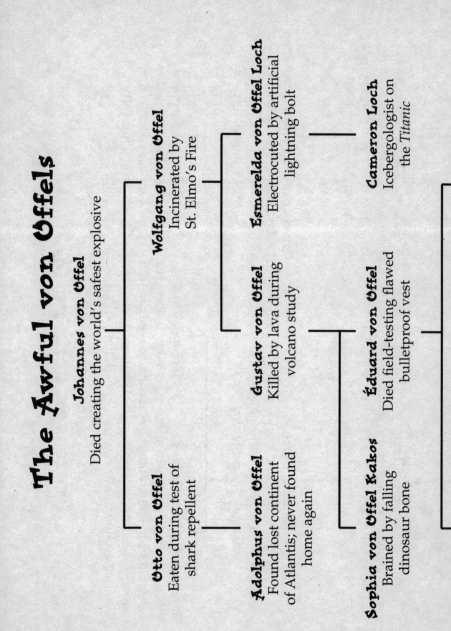

The Awful von Offels

Johannes von Offel
Died creating the world's safest explosive

Wolfgang von Offel
Incinerated by St. Elmo's Fire

Otto von Offel
Eaten during test of shark repellent

Esmerelda von Offel Loch
Electrocuted by artificial lightning bolt

Gustav von Offel
Killed by lava during volcano study

Adolphus von Offel
Found lost continent of Atlantis; never found home again

Cameron Loch
Icebergologist on the *Titanic*

Éduard von Offel
Died field-testing flawed bulletproof vest

Sophia von Offel Kakos
Brained by falling dinosaur bone

Rula von Offel Malle
Evaporated

Kurt von Offel
Weak batteries in antigravity backpack

Beatrice Malle O'Door
Drowned pursuing the Loch Ness Monster

Colin von Offel
Transplanted his brain into wildebeest

Felicity von Offel Day
Brained by diving bell during deep-sea exploration

Feldspar O'Door
Died of freezer burn during cryogenics experiment

Alan von Offel
Failed to survive field test of nonpoisonous arsenic

Professor John von Offel (?)

Johannes von Offel's
Book of Scientific Observations, 1891

My next-door neighbor and colleague, Jedidiah Flask, has just returned from the hospital. He was rushed there immediately after partaking of my hospitality and quaffing a large cup of hot chocolate that I had fortified with coal dust. Jedidiah looks not at all well. I am therefore forced to admit that my hypothesis about the healthy properties of eating coal may be in error. It seemed so logical that a strong fossil fuel should power the body just as it powers a furnace or a locomotive. How disappointing that coal should be proved poisonous. However, I am not deterred in my belief that nutrition is the answer to the question of extended life.

CHAPTER 1

Brainless Beasts

Professor John von Offel yanked open the door to Einstein Elementary School as the first bell rang on Monday morning. He strode quickly down the hall, unaware of the charred bits of wood that dropped from his wiry hair and rumpled suit.

The battered parrot on the professor's shoulder picked his way carefully over the smoking bits. "You and your crazy experiments!" said the parrot. "Next time you try to harness the sun's energy, let me know *before* you turn our house into a three-alarm fire!"

"The Arcana Fire Department proved themselves quite capable of dousing the flames," said the professor. He dismissed the parrot's concern with a wave of his left hand, which was missing its pinky finger. "Besides, two rooms in the west wing are a small sacrifice to make in the name of science, Atom. In a few more minutes, I would have been able to fortify my body with the sun's life-giving rays!"

"A few more minutes and the whole house would have burned down!" Atom replied. "You're lucky any part of the house is left standing, after all the reckless experiments you von Offels have tried there." The parrot plucked a charred wood chip from his bedraggled feathers. "I've seen everything from artificial lightning bolts to Saint Elmo's fire! My tail feathers are still singed from that mishap with the world's safest explosive you were working on."

"Don't be such a selfish squab," said the

professor. "At least you're still alive. Fully, wonderfully alive. Don't you wish the same for me?"

"So you've got a point," the parrot said. "But why don't you try *safe* science for a change? Look at you! You smell like a barbecue, and you're still part ghost! Not to mention that now we're late for Ethan Flask's science class. Didn't Mr. Flask say he's bringing in a new animal for his intelligence studies?"

"Bah! You'd have made a good Flask yourself," scoffed the professor. "I don't know why you're so eager to listen to that nobody when you've got a true scientific genius staring you in the face."

Atom looked into the professor's flashing eyes and shivered. "Being dead for a century hasn't helped your looks any. Have you seen yourself in the mirror lately?"

"Shhh!" said the professor, glancing up and down the deserted hallway. "You know very well I can't see my reflection until I have regained the missing 35 percent of my body. And as for Flask's animal studies, I should think you'd want to keep away from those creatures. Most of them seem to dislike you intensely. Although Flask does look for intelligence in the most irritatingly brainless beasts."

Fear flashed across von Offel's face. He stopped in midstep. "You don't think Flask would bring in another orangutan, do you?" the professor asked.

"Like the one that thought you were his girl-friend?" Atom laughed so hard he had to come in for a landing on the professor's shoulder. "I wish I had a photo —"

The parrot broke into a loud squawk as the school's principal, Dr. Kepler, came through the gym door. She stopped in front of the professor and glanced curiously at Atom.

"Good morning, Professor von Offel. I hope you haven't forgotten about the science fair later this week," she said with a smile. "Mr. Klumpp is just getting the gym ready now."

"Science fair?" The professor glanced toward

the gym, where the school custodian was furiously mopping. "I'm rather busy."

Before he could continue, Mr. Klumpp rushed over with his mop. "I just spent an hour cleaning the floors," he grumbled. "Where did all this burnt wood come from?"

Professor von Offel shrugged, sending a shower of charred bits to the floor. "Er, there was a slight mishap at my house this morning."

"I'll say — I mean, awk!" cried Atom. "A slight mishap. Awk!"

"Nothing to be concerned about," the professor continued. He turned to leave, but Mr. Klumpp blocked his path.

"Every mess is my concern," Mr. Klumpp insisted. He pulled a mini vacuum from his supply cart. "This will just take a second."

Mr. Klumpp flipped the switch. He didn't notice the three sixth graders who sped past the gym door on their way to class.

"I can't believe I got up at six o'clock this

morning, and I'm *still* late for science lab!" moaned Prescott Forrester III.

Alberta Wong and Luis Antilla, his best friends and fellow lab assistants, jogged down the hall next to him.

"Our trial run this morning took longer than we thought," Alberta said. "But it's good training for next week's mini marathon."

"Yeah," Luis agreed. "Thanks for being our timekeeper, Prescott."

Prescott shrugged. "I just hope we don't get in trouble with Mr. Flask for being late."

"*I* just hope Mr. Flask doesn't get in trouble with Professor von Offel," Luis said. "It won't look good if Mr. Flask's three lab assistants can't even get to class on time. What if Professor von Offel uses that as an excuse to recommend that Mr. Flask not receive the Vanguard Teacher Award?"

"This is the first time that we've ever been late. I don't think Professor von Offel will hold that against Mr. Flask," Alberta said.

"The guy's not exactly predictable," Prescott

pointed out. He hiked his backpack straps higher on his shoulders. "So far, we've seen him walk through flour and leave no footprints, never mind walk into a train and totally disappear!"

Alberta's eyes gleamed. "Talk about fascinating. I'm so glad I picked the von Offels to do my science fair project on."

"If you ask me, the von Offels belong in a circus freak show, not a science fair," Luis said sarcastically. "But if your project helps Mr. Flask score points with the professor, I guess it's a good thing."

"You guess?" said Alberta. "That's not exactly a wholehearted endorse —"

"We're in luck!" Prescott interrupted. He stopped just outside the open door to the sixth-grade science lab. "Professor von Offel isn't here yet."

"It's not like Professor von Offel to skip class." Alberta looked around the lab curiously as she and Luis raced in behind Prescott. "I wonder where he is?"

CHAPTER 2

Polly Want a Cracker?

"**P**hew!" sighed Atom. He bobbed along on the professor's shoulder as von Offel walked away from the gym. "I thought we'd never escape that one-man neatness patrol. I was afraid Mr. Klumpp might vacuum up what little substance your body has!"

The professor turned to meet the parrot's beady gaze. "This is no laughing matter, Atom.

How long must I wait until that unwitting eager beaver Flask provides the inspiration I need to become fully human once more?"

"Hark!" Atom cupped an outstretched wing around his ear. "I think I hear the unwitting eager beaver now."

The science teacher's voice carried clearly through the open door of the lab just ahead.

"Before I begin today's lab," Mr. Flask was saying, "I'd like to hand back last week's Detective Science quizzes."

A second voice, louder and shriller than Mr. Flask's, echoed: "*Ack!* Before I begin today's lab, I'd like to hand back last week's —"

The rest of the echo was drowned out by laughter. The whole class was roaring hysterically.

Out in the hall, Professor von Offel frowned at Atom. "What kind of idiotic — ?"

He strode through the doorway, only to find himself right next to Mr. Flask and his newest animal subject.

"A parrot?" Professor von Offel stopped so suddenly that Atom nearly toppled beak first from his shoulder.

"Hey! I mean — awk!" Atom recovered his balance, then stared long and hard at the other parrot.

"Don't tell me Atom is jealous," laughed Mr. Flask. He grinned and held up the bright green parrot perched on his finger. "Atom, I'd like you to meet a creature who might very well be a long-lost cousin of yours. This is Gary."

A low, growling squawk rumbled at the back of Atom's throat. Taking off from the professor's shoulder, Atom flew in a slow circle around the lab. For once, he took no note of the angry hisses and growls that came from the animal cages at the front of the room. All his attention was focused on the parrot perched on Mr. Flask's finger.

"You call this animal intelligent?" Professor von Offel stared down his long, hooked nose at Gary. Then he laughed in Mr. Flask's face.

"To be sure, many parrots possess an uncanny knack for repeating words and phrases."

"Ack! To be sure!" mimicked Gary. "Many parrots possess an uncanny knack for repeating words and phrases. Ack!"

All the sixth graders burst out laughing.

"Talk about a perfect imitation!" Alberta called out. "Gary sounded just like you, Professor!"

"He captured the pompous, lecturing tone exactly," Luis added under his breath. "The whole class will fall asleep if Gary keeps it up."

"Shhh!" Alberta shot a withering glance at Luis.

"As I was saying," the professor droned on, in the same flat voice, "the ability to repeat a few words or phrases is merely mimicry. It's a far cry from the real intelligence required to truly speak, not just repeat what you've heard with no understanding of what you're saying."

Atom picked his way up the professor's collar until his beak was right in the professor's ear. "Thanks a heap!" he whispered.

"Well, that's not the whole picture, Professor," Mr. Flask said brightly.

The professor fished an ancient monocle from his jacket pocket and stared through it at Mr. Flask. "Indeed?" he inquired in an openly doubtful voice.

The students' eyes bounced back and forth like tennis balls as Mr. Flask and Professor von Offel argued.

"Absolutely," Mr. Flask replied. "Studies suggest that the ability to learn a spoken language does indicate a highly sophisticated level of intelligence in animals, even if the animal is just repeating what it hears." Mr. Flask's lab coat billowed behind him as he carried Gary over to the lab table. Gary hopped off his finger onto the table and stood calmly, preening his wing feathers.

"The ability to *imitate* spoken language is not the same as the ability to *generate* language," the professor said haughtily.

"True," said Mr. Flask. "But imitation could mean some kind of intelligence. Take Gary here as an example," Mr. Flask continued. "Everyone knows parrots possess the ability to imitate spoken language. But some parrots are able to learn more words and repeat more complex sentence structures than others."

Mr. Flask glanced casually at Atom, who glared at Gary, jealously.

"Is talking a lot a sign of intelligence in people, too?" Max Hoof spoke up from his desk in the second row.

Next to him, Sean Baxter sat up straighter in his seat. "If it is, then I must be a genius," he muttered.

"Being talkative doesn't necessarily show special intelligence in humans," Mr. Flask said. "But re-creating complex sentence patterns *is* a sign of superior intelligence in animals. And I've heard Gary imitate entire conversations!"

Gary immediately let out a squawk. "Ack! Re-creating complex sentence patterns is a sign of superior intelligence in animals," he mimicked. "Ack!"

"Wow," said Alberta. "He's good, all right."

"Yeah, right," mumbled Atom. Then he covered with a squawk. "Awk! He's good, all right!"

Mr. Flask grinned. "Glad you agree, Atom," he said. "Even Gary's name indicates how talkative he is. It's short for *garrulous.*"

"What does that mean?" Prescott wanted to know.

"Garrulous means excessively talkative, for those of you who are wondering," said Mr. Flask. "The name suits Gary perfectly because he hardly ever stops talking. Gary's language skills go far beyond your average 'Polly wants a cracker.'"

"Ack!" screeched Gary. "Polly wants a cracker! Ack!"

Atom let out a choked cough.

"Is that the best that showoff ball of feathers can do?" Atom whispered in the professor's ear. "I'll show him!"

The professor shook his head vigorously back and forth, but Atom ignored the warning.

With a devilish glint in his beady eyes, he squawked, "Awk! Polly wants a *nacho grande con queso* with extra onions!"

CHAPTER 3

Dueling Parrots

All the kids in science lab stared at Atom with their mouths hanging open.

"Whoa!" said Heather Patterson. "Nobody said anything about a *nacho grande*. Where did Atom get that from?"

"He *talked*," Luis said. He exchanged meaningful glances with Alberta and Prescott. "Not like an animal — like a person! And this isn't the first time, either. We've heard him before."

Professor von Offel glared at the three lab assistants. Before Atom could say another word, the professor squeezed his beak shut.

"Mr. Flask, I'm surprised that you encourage this sort of overactive speculation in your students," the professor said sternly. "It's highly unscientific."

Mr. Flask's smile faded. "I encourage originality but always with careful scientific methodology," he said.

He turned to Luis. "It may have *seemed* as if Atom were talking on his own. But I'm sure there's a *scientific* explanation for what just happened. We all know parrots don't have the ability to speak without being prompted. And from what I've witnessed here in science lab" — Mr. Flask arched an eyebrow as he glanced at Atom — "Atom's skills are limited at best."

Professor von Offel just barely managed to stop Atom from dive-bombing Mr. Flask with his sharp talons extended.

"Er, Atom possesses no skills beyond those of any ordinary parrot. None whatsoever," the professor said, keeping a firm grip on his parrot. "As it happens, I was considering having a *nacho grande* for lunch today. Atom simply overheard me and then mimicked my words here in class."

"You were talking about it out loud?" asked Max. "To yourself?"

Professor von Offel opened his mouth, then closed it again and walked stiffly to his desk at the back of the room. "Mr. Flask, I would advise you to instruct your students to be more respectful."

"Yes, of course," Mr. Flask agreed. His eyes sparkled with challenge as he gazed back and forth between Gary and Atom. "But perhaps you would agree to a contest, Professor? In the interest of science?"

His students all leaned forward. "What kind of contest?" Alberta asked.

"A talking parrot contest!" Mr. Flask answered. "Having two parrots in the classroom presents us with an opportunity to compare how well they can learn spoken language. We'll test Gary and Atom with a series of words and phrases."

"And whichever parrot repeats the most words correctly wins!" Alberta finished. "It's brilliant!"

"We could have the contest at the end of the week, right after the science fair," said Mr. Flask. "That would give Professor von Offel and me a chance to prepare Atom and Gary for the event."

Mr. Flask held out a hand and walked toward the professor. "What do you say? Shall we shake on it?" he asked.

The professor fumbled with his inkwell and quill pen, taking longer than usual to set them up on his desk. "Well, um —" he mumbled.

"Do it!" Atom hissed in the professor's ear. The parrot glowered at Gary from atop the professor's shoulder. "I mean shake on it. Awk! Shake on it."

"Unless there's some reason you don't want

Atom to compete with Gary?" Mr. Flask asked.

"Er —" The professor fidgeted some more with his inkwell before he finally met Mr. Flask's gaze. "There's no reason. No reason at all," he said.

Reluctantly, von Offel reached out and shook Mr. Flask's hand. In a flat, quiet voice he said, "I accept your challenge."

"Excellent!" Ethan said.

The sixth graders burst into cheers and applause. Atom paraded back and forth on the professor's desk, flexing his wings and pumping up his green chest feathers.

"Atom looks like he's ready to start his training right now!" laughed Heather.

"I'm ready, too — for something to eat!" Prescott added. "All that talk about *queso* and extra onions gave me a nacho craving!"

"It sure beats the mystery meat in the cafeteria," Luis said. "But I'd rather have a big, heaping bowl of pasta."

"Mmmm. Me, too," Alberta said dreamily. "After all, carbo loading is an important part of our training for the mini marathon."

Prescott rolled his eyes. "I don't see what the big deal is about carbo loading," he said. "How can a bunch of noodles make you run better? And don't some people think you should eat a lot of protein before a race anyhow?"

"Excellent questions, Prescott!" Mr. Flask said as he left the professor's desk and wound his way to the front of the class. "Alberta, Luis, do you have any ideas?"

Alberta's hand shot into the air. "Our bodies need extra energy for long-distance events like marathons," she said. "And when it comes to providing energy, all foods are *not* created equal."

"Right," said Luis. He took out his science notebook and a pencil. "Foods that are rich in complex carbohydrates, like pasta and rice and potatoes, supply the most energy to our muscles. That's why athletes need to load up on those foods for peak performance."

"So a *nacho grande* rates lower than a bowl of rice?" Prescott shook his head and groaned. "Remind me never to become a sports fanatic, okay?"

Mr. Flask consoled Prescott with a pat on the shoulder. "Unfortunately," he said, "the foods we think are the yummiest, like nachos . . ."

"And ice cream!" Max called out.

"And ice cream," Mr. Flask agreed, "fatty, sugary foods like these only give us short-term energy. But our bodies process complex carbohydrates into glucose that can be used for energy by the muscles for a lot longer, sometimes for hours."

"Wow." Heather licked her lips. "I never knew food could be so scientific."

Mr. Flask nodded. "Oh, but it is!" he said. As he looked out over his class, his eyes lit up like a neon sign.

"Heather, you've just given me a very *tasty*

idea. As of today, we're starting a new study unit," he said. "On the science of food!"

"Sounds yummy!" said Alberta.

Excited murmurs rippled through the room.

"Food? So," Sean said, "if I come in tomorrow and say my dog ate my homework —"

"You don't even *have* a dog, Sean," Prescott pointed out.

"Edible homework will certainly be part of our study unit," laughed Mr. Flask. "But that's just part of the science of food."

As he went to the chalkboard, his students all reached for their pens and notebooks. Even Professor von Offel nodded his head with interest.

Excellent, Mr. Flask thought. Sure, the professor and I have had our differences. But perhaps food science is the topic that will finally get us to see eye to eye.

CHAPTER 4

Klumpp vs. Ketchup

M r. Flask sat in the teachers' lounge after school with his laptop computer open on the table in front of him.

"Hmm." He shuffled through the pile of notebooks and index cards he'd brought with him, all containing experiments he'd collected over the years.

"Should I try the Ketchup Diver or the Density Stacker, or maybe the Edible Earth?" he murmured.

"Ack! The Ketchup Diver," Gary squawked from his cage on the table. He stood on his perch, munching sunflower seeds. "Or the Density Stacker or maybe the Edible Earth. Ack!"

"Good work, Gary," said Mr. Flask as he started to type on his computer. "We'll start training in earnest as soon as I've —"

Wham!

The door to the lounge banged open, and Mr. Klumpp stomped in.

"Phew!" The custodian threw himself onto the couch, pulled a handkerchief from his back pocket, and wiped the bald, sweaty crown of his head. "What a job!"

Mr. Flask raised his eyebrows, an expression of sudden concern in his eyes. "My marmoset didn't escape and turn over all the trash cans again, did it?" he asked. "I placed an extra hook on the cage and —"

"It wasn't your animals," Mr. Klumpp muttered. "For once."

The custodian reached for a paper cup from

the water cooler, then stopped with his hand in midair when he saw Gary's cage.

"I've been cleaning and polishing and mopping for a week, getting the gym ready for the science fair," grumbled the custodian, glaring at the parrot. "I've spruced up the whole school so it will look nice for the parents."

"Bravo! We all appreciate your hard work, Mr. Klumpp." Mr. Flask jumped up and swept away some seed hulls that Gary had dropped outside the cage. "Please don't worry about Gary. I'll tidy up after him and —"

"Excuse me," Alberta interrupted. She appeared in the doorway with a camera hanging by its strap from her neck.

Prescott and Luis were with her. All three lab assistants glanced with curiosity around the faculty lounge.

"Is Professor von Offel here?" Alberta asked.

Ethan shook his head. "I'm afraid not," he answered.

"Oh." Alberta frowned and pointed to her camera. "I wanted to take his picture for my science fair project. It's a display on the history of the von Offels," she said. "Including all the awards they've won and their brilliant contributions to science."

Luis rolled his eyes.

"You mean, the many treacheries the awful von Offels committed just to make themselves rich and famous," he said. He stepped into the lounge and pointed to the papers scattered around Mr. Flask's laptop computer. "You're a much more conscientious, *serious* scientist than any von Offel, Mr. Flask."

"Thanks for the vote of confidence, Luis," Mr. Flask said. "But remember, a good scientist never makes judgments without concrete proof."

Prescott looked past Luis at the words that were typed out on Mr. Flask's computer screen. "A ketchup submarine experiment? Is that going to be part of our unit on food science?"

"Ketchup?" Mr. Klumpp sat bolt upright on the couch. "Food science?" he hissed. His eyes bulged from their sockets. "I just spent a whole week cleaning the school, and you're going to do experiments with" — he squeezed his paper cup, sending a miniature waterfall onto the couch and floor — "*food*?!"

"It's not nearly as messy as it sounds," Mr. Flask said quickly. "I can assure you we'll do our best to —"

"You can't be serious!" Mr. Klumpp jumped to his feet, his face turning a deep, mottled purple. "You, Mr. Flask, are a — a lunatic!"

"Look who's talking," Luis mumbled under his breath.

Gary let out a squawk from his cage. "Ack! Lunatic! Lunatic!" he screeched.

"Who said that?" Mr. Klumpp demanded, whirling around.

"I'd say that's our cue to get out of here," whispered Prescott. He backed toward the doorway. "Fast!"

He whirled around and took off down the hall with Alberta and Luis right behind him.

"Try the professor's office!" Ethan called out after them. Then he slipped between the custodian and Gary's cage. "I can explain, Mr. Klumpp —"

CHAPTER 5

Searching for Professor von Offel

"I have a bad feeling about this, guys." Prescott pulled Alberta and Luis to a stop just down the hall from Professor von Offel's office. "Every time we go to that office, something weird happens."

Alberta shrugged. "All we have to do is find Professor von Offel and take his picture for my project. It'll be simple."

"*Nothing* about Professor von Offel is simple," Prescott insisted. "Don't you remember the first time we saw him in his office? He disappeared!"

"Well, I guess strange stuff is part of the territory when you're a ghost," Luis pointed out. "Especially when you're a sneaky *von Offel* ghost. That's why we should keep an eye on the professor. Maybe we'll finally get some concrete *scientific* proof to convince Mr. Flask."

"How, exactly, do we get scientific proof about something that most people don't even think is real?" said Prescott. "Ghosts aren't exactly part of our science curriculum, you know."

Luis shrugged. "We've seen Professor von Offel disappear. We've seen him walk into a train. We know he doesn't leave fingerprints or footprints." He ticked off the evidence on his fingers. "Sooner or later, the proof will add up so that even a scientist like Mr. Flask has to believe it."

With purposeful steps, Luis strode down the hall toward Professor von Offel's office.

"You're right," Alberta agreed, hurrying after Luis with Prescott. "About the ghost part, anyway. But I don't agree with you about Professor von Offel being sneaky. Maybe he's a ghost, but he's not a crooked ghost."

"Oh, please," Luis scoffed. "All the von Offels were sneaks, *including* the professor. He's so crooked he probably has to twist his clothes on in the morning."

Alberta shook her head firmly. "He's a brilliant scientist. I can't wait to see his face when I tell him my science fair project is about his family," she said.

"If he's even visible when we get there," Luis said.

"Shhh!" Prescott put a finger to his lips and stopped just outside the open doorway to the professor's office. "He might hear you!" he whispered.

Stepping past him, Alberta peered through the doorway and frowned. The swivel chair at the professor's cluttered desk was empty.

"He's not here," she reported. "The light's

32

on, though. And his briefcase is on the desk. He can't be far aw —"

"Fascinating!" said a voice from behind the desk.

Alberta took a tentative step into the office, and then another. "Hello?" she said.

No one answered.

As she angled around the desk, the first thing Alberta saw was Atom. The parrot paced across a thick dictionary that lay open on the floor. He seemed to be scouring it, keeping his beak close to the page. The professor was behind the parrot — on his hands and knees in a small alcove that held a coffee machine and a miniature refrigerator.

"Professor von Offel?" said Alberta.

Neither the parrot nor the professor gave any sign that they noticed the three students. While Atom read, the professor pulled open the refrigerator door and then closed it again. Four times he repeated the process, watching with rapt attention.

"Fascinating," he said for the second time. "One *presumes* the light goes off. But as the door is *closed*, one can never know with certainty."

"See?" Prescott raised his index finger and made small circles next to his temple. "Didn't I warn you?" he whispered.

Alberta frowned. She stepped firmly forward and said in a loud voice, "Professor von Offel? It's me, Alberta Wong."

Professor von Offel looked up at the three lab assistants in surprise. "What do you want?" he asked sharply.

"Well," said Alberta with her brightest smile, "I'm doing my science fair project on the von Offel family, and —"

The professor jumped to his feet and jabbed a finger at her camera. "Is that one of those newfangled photographic imaging devices?" he cried. "How *dare* you bring it here!"

Alberta's smile evaporated. Behind her, Prescott leaned close to Luis and whispered, "I don't think that was quite the reaction she was hoping for."

"I j-just want to take your picture," Alberta said, "for my —"

"No!" shrieked the professor, waving his arms wildly. "Absolutely not! Leave me alone, you meddlesome brats."

Alberta still didn't give up. "It'll only take a second," she said. "I'll just take one shot and —"

"Get . . . out!" bellowed the professor. "NOW!"

Luis and Prescott yanked Alberta out of the office just in time. The last thing they saw before the door slammed shut was the professor's face, mottled with rage, as he lunged toward them with outstretched arms.

Atom watched through the door's glass window as the three lab assistants ran down the hall, terrified.

"Nice going, Johannes," squawked the parrot. "After that little temper tantrum those nosy kids will be more suspicious than ever!"

"Bah!" The professor sank weakly into his swivel chair. As he tried to catch his breath, his face and hands faded in and out of sight. "You know very well my body does not yet have enough substance to project an image on film," he said. "I couldn't let them take my photograph."

"Would it kill to you to be polite every once in a while?" Atom asked.

"What for?" The professor waved away the suggestion. "The von Offels didn't get ahead by being polite. That sort of nonsense is for weak-spirited fools like the Flasks."

Atom flew back to the dictionary and pecked at the small print. "Well, don't blame me when those kids start snooping around even more," he squawked. "I won't have time to watch your back while I'm training for the challenge with Gary."

"Ah, yes. The challenge," the professor murmured. The corners of his mouth twitched up into a half smile. "That overgrown canary is in for a big surprise when he faces off with you, Atom."

Out in the hall, Alberta, Prescott, and Luis kept running. They didn't slow their pace until after they had pushed through the front doors and were outside Einstein Elementary.

"Enough! I feel like I just ran a mini marathon — and I'm not even in training!" Prescott threw himself down onto the grassy lawn, gasping for breath. He groaned when he saw Luis and Alberta jogging in place next to him. "I don't believe it. You guys didn't even break a sweat!"

Luis angled a glance back at Einstein Elementary. "Professor von Offel is such a jerk!" he exclaimed. "He didn't have to be so mean."

"Too bad." Prescott groaned as he pushed

himself to a seated position on the grass. "It would have been great to have a picture of the last living von Offel for your project, Alberta."

Alberta turned to her friends with a mysterious smile. "Who says I won't?" she asked.

CHAPTER 6

Candid Camera

"**C**ome on, guys," said Alberta. She patted the camera that was hidden beneath her zip-up sweatshirt. "If Professor von Offel won't pose for a photograph to use in my science fair project, I'll just have to settle for a few candid shots."

She moved away from the glow of a streetlight and onto the tree-lined block where Professor von Offel lived. Prescott and Luis, right behind her, had to blink to see Alberta in the darkening evening shadows.

"I can't believe I let you talk me into this!" Prescott whispered. "My stomach is twisting into a zillion knots just thinking about what the professor will do if he catches us."

"That's probably the nachos you ate for dinner," Luis teased. "When are you going to learn that carbo loading is the way to go?"

"When are you guys going to learn that sneaking around could get us into serious hot water?" Prescott shot back.

Up ahead, the professor's battered Victorian mansion came into view. Luis frowned at the burned-out windows and overgrown, weed-infested yard. "I don't care about that von Offel lunatic," he said. "But I hope Mr. Flask doesn't see us. I doubt he would consider sneaking around to be appropriate scientific behavior for his lab assistants."

Alberta winced as she glanced at Mr. Flask's Foucault's pendulum, the solar panels fitted onto his roof, and the rooftop bubble that contained his telescope. "Okay, so I'm not being very scientific," she admitted. "But I need these pictures for my project. And I'm going to get them!"

She pressed a finger to her lips. Keeping close to the bushes, she tiptoed into the alley that separated Mr. Flask's house from the professor's.

"Check it out," Prescott whispered. He nodded over the neatly trimmed azaleas beneath Mr. Flask's kitchen window. "Mr. Flask is training Gary."

Luis and Alberta glanced past the parasailing equipment and souped-up racing bike that were stored next to the alley. In the brightly lit kitchen, Mr. Flask read from a stack of index cards.

"O-oh, say can you see by the dawn's early light —"

The parrot's feathered head bobbed as he squawked, "O-oh, say can you see! Ack! By the dawn's early light —"

"Good!" Their teacher's encouraging voice

floated through the window. "You're doing great, Gary."

"Ack! Doing great, Gary! You're doing great!" mimicked the parrot.

Luis's teeth glowed white in the darkness as he turned to grin at his friends. "Man, that contest is in the bag!" he whispered.

"Shhh!" warned Alberta.

She tiptoed farther down the alley, keeping her eyes on the von Offel house. Most of the windows were dark, dusty, and covered with cobwebs. Several held broken panes of glass; others were covered with peeling, splintered shutters.

Luis shook his head in disgust. "Talk about a disaster area. The place looks totally abandoned."

"Not quite." Alberta's eyes gleamed as she nodded toward the lighted windows of one small wing of the house. "There's Atom," she whispered.

The parrot stood on a perch in a dusty room that held little more than an armchair, a lamp, a table, and several sheet-covered lumps of furniture. Next to him, a vinyl disc spun on an old-fashioned record player with a speaker horn attached to it.

"When was the last time you saw someone use a record player?" Prescott whispered. "Doesn't the professor know about CDs?"

"He's a ghost, remember?" said Luis. "Being dead for a couple of decades could make it hard to catch up on the digital age. Anyway, the professor's not using the record player. Atom is."

The three sixth graders stood watching the parrot. Strains of opera wafted through the open window. Atom's green-feathered body waved back and forth in time to the music. His beak moved nonstop as he sang along with the record.

"He's singing opera — in *Italian*," Alberta whispered. Her jaw dropped open. "How can he memorize all that? Professor von Offel isn't even in the room to prompt him."

"Atom's not really singing. He's just

beaking the words!" Prescott said. He bit his lip uncertainly. "Right?"

"Something's up with that bird," Luis mumbled, turning to Prescott in the dark alley. "The way he talks — and didn't it look like he was actually *reading* that dictionary in the professor's office this afternoon?"

"Forget about Atom. There's the professor!" Alberta's excited whisper came from just ahead.

Alberta pointed to a lighted window two rooms away from the parlor where Atom continued to belt out Italian opera. The professor sat at the kitchen table, sipping a cup of tea while he flipped through the pages of a magazine.

"You're in luck, Alberta," whispered Prescott. He plucked nervously at his shirt while Alberta crouched next to the scruffy, overgrown hedge that edged the alleyway. "Just don't get caught!"

Alberta lifted her camera and looked through the viewfinder. A flash of light winked into the night as she took her first photograph.

"Don't look up," whispered Prescott. "Just keep reading, Professor."

Inside the kitchen, the professor sipped his tea. He didn't so much as glance up from the magazine on the table in front of him.

Alberta kept snapping photos until she had finished the entire roll. When she lowered her camera a minute later, she was beaming.

"Gotcha," she whispered.

CHAPTER 7

Hard-boiled Disaster

L uis and Prescott were already sitting at their desks when Alberta walked into the science lab the next morning.

"I just dropped off my film at the Foto Bin in town," Alberta said, before slipping into her seat. "It'll be ready after school."

"Cool." Prescott gave her the thumbs-up sign. "I'm glad you got the photos without Professor von Offel biting our heads off."

Alberta gazed reverently at the professor, sitting at his desk at the back of the lab. "He's not so bad. Scientific geniuses are moody, that's all," she said.

"Professor von Offel looked like he would have ripped your head off with his bare hands if Prescott and I hadn't dragged you out of his office yesterday," Luis whispered. "That's more than just moody, Alberta. It's —"

"Good morning, everyone!" Mr. Flask walked briskly into the lab and set Gary's cage on top of the experiment table. "I hope you're all ready for some hard-boiled food science."

"I hope you're all ready — ack!" squawked Gary. "For some hard-boiled food science."

"*O, sole mio!*" Atom sang from his perch on the professor's desk.

Heather turned to look at Atom, crinkling up her nose. "Is he singing?" she asked. "In Italian?"

"Certainly not!" The professor tried to grab Atom's beak, but Atom took off. He flapped across the lab to the experiment table, where he landed right next to Gary's cage.

Atom poked his beak between the wires of the cage and let out a raspberry with his tongue. "Take that!" he squawked. "I mean — awk! Hard-boiled science. I hope you're all ready. Awk!"

"Bravo, Atom! Bravo, Gary!" laughed Mr. Flask. "But let's save the competition for the end of the week, shall we?"

He covered Gary's cage with a sheet and then turned back to the class. Reaching into the pockets of his lab coat, he pulled out two eggs. His eyes sparkled with challenge as he held the eggs up.

"One of these is hard-boiled, and the other is raw," said Mr. Flask. "Can anyone tell me which is which?"

"They look exactly the same to me," Max called out. "Is this a trick question?"

"Not at all!" said Mr. Flask. He grabbed a couple of egg cartons from the experiment table and gave them to Alberta, Prescott, and

Luis. "Once our lab assistants hand out these eggs, you'll see that there's a very simple, scientific way of determining which ones are hard-boiled and which ones are raw."

Sean took an egg from Luis and weighed it in his palm. "Throw them at someone?" Sean suggested, raising his eyebrows hopefully.

"I'm afraid a food fight won't be part of our food science unit, Sean," Mr. Flask said dryly. He chuckled as disappointed groans echoed throughout the room. "Try spinning the egg like a top," he suggested.

Sean placed his egg on end and twirled it. "Hey!" he said, frowning. "Mine won't spin. It just wobbles all over the place."

"Mine, too," said a half dozen other students.

"This one spins fine," Heather spoke up. The egg on her desk twirled perfectly on its axis.

"So does mine," said Alberta. She caught the spinning egg in her hand and held it up. "I bet this one is hard-boiled."

"Definitely," Luis agreed. He looked down at his own egg, which wobbled unsteadily across his desk. "And mine is raw."

Mr. Flask applauded them. "Absolutely right! How could you tell?" he asked.

"Well, maybe since the hard-boiled egg is solid, the whole egg spins at the same speed," Alberta began.

"Right you are," said Mr. Flask. "The liquid inside a raw egg can't keep up with the spinning shell. Since different parts of the egg are spinning at different speeds, that throws the egg off balance."

Murmurs of comprehension rose from the other students. At the back of the room, Professor von Offel stared through an antique monocle at his own egg, which spun perfectly on his desktop.

"Interesting," he murmured.

"Score one for Mr. Flask," whispered Prescott. "Professor von Offel looks like he's really into this experiment."

"What does he need a magnifying glass for?" Luis wondered. "Did you see how thick the glass is?"

Prescott had to choke back a laugh. "It makes his eye look like a bulging Ping-Pong ball that could pop out of his head any second," he whispered.

"I heard that." Alberta turned in her seat and glowered at them. "You don't have to make fun of —"

She jumped as the door to the science lab banged open and Mr. Klumpp barged in.

"What is the meaning of this!" the custodian demanded. "You're using eggs? When I've been working overtime to make Einstein Elementary shine?"

"We're not *breaking* the eggs," Mr. Flask assured him.

"Anyway, this one's hard-boiled, so you don't have anything to worry about." Alberta held up her egg with a reassuring smile. "Want to see how it —"

"No!" Mr. Klumpp snatched the egg from Alberta's hand.

"Mr. Klumpp," said Ethan, "there's really no need to —"

"I put up with your exploding volcanoes," sputtered Mr. Klumpp. He stormed around the room, grabbing every egg in sight. "I cleaned up after your rock meteorites blasted flour all over the lab —"

"You mean, all over us," Prescott said under his breath.

"But," Mr. Klumpp continued, "I draw the line at eggs being splattered all over *my* school!"

His arms loaded down with eggs, the custodian marched toward the door.

"You missed one, Mr. Klumpp," Heather called out.

Mr. Klumpp stopped short, scouring the room with angry, bulging eyes. "Aha!" he said as his gaze zeroed in on the egg that wobbled in unsteady circles on Prescott's desk. "Throw it to me."

"But —" Prescott shook his head. "I don't think you want —"

"Throw it to me!" Mr. Klumpp insisted. He cradled the eggs he had collected in one arm and held out his other hand expectantly. "Now!"

Prescott shrugged. "If you say so."

He tossed the egg at the custodian.

Crack!

It smashed into the pyramid of eggs cradled in Mr. Klumpp's arms.

Crack! Splat! Plop!

Gooey raw egg splattered all over the custodian's shirt and pants. A puddle of yellow goo spread out on the floor around him. Hard-boiled eggs rolled through the raw yolks, sending trails of yellow across the lab.

"Ooooh!" Mr. Klumpp seethed. His hands balled into tight fists as he stared at the mess. "I — I won't forget this, Mr. Flask!"

He clomped out the door, leaving a trail of sticky yellow boot prints.

"Well, class." Mr. Flask shrugged, staring after the custodian. "I guess it's just as well that I didn't mention the next experiment we'll be trying."

"What's that?" asked Max.

Mr. Flask grinned and pulled mixes for gelatin, pudding, and pie crust from underneath the experiment table. "Edible Earth!"

CHAPTER 8

Impossible!

"I really shouldn't be eating this if I'm in training for the mini marathon. But who can resist chocolate cookie crunch?" Alberta licked ice cream from her cone as she, Prescott, and Luis slid into a booth at the Real Scoop in downtown Arcana. "I'll bet anything my time on my next practice run is going to be off," she said.

"It'll be worth it," said Luis, biting into his

hot fudge sundae. "This tastes a lot better than a baked potato."

"It's like I've been trying to tell you," said Prescott. "*Sugar* loading is the way to go, guys. Not carbo loading."

"Sweet, but not nutritionally sound, Prescott," said Luis.

"Well, mixing up all that pudding and gelatin for our Edible Earth experiment definitely gave me a craving for something sweet," Prescott replied.

"Me, too," Alberta chimed in. "I can't wait until tomorrow when the Edible Earth will be ready to eat. I guess I can always stoke up on pasta later."

Prescott drank half his double chocolate shake in a single slurp before banging the glass down on the table. "Alberta, where did you put the photos we just picked up?" he asked.

"Right here." She pulled a Foto Bin envelope from her backpack. She spread the photos out on the table, and all three sixth graders leaned forward to examine them.

"Wait a minute," Prescott said, frowning. "The professor isn't even in these pictures!"

Alberta's eyes went wide as she flipped through the photos once, then again. "There's the professor's house," she murmured. "And there's the lighted kitchen window. We know the professor was sitting right there. We saw him! So why isn't he in the pictures?"

"Do you think you aimed wrong?" wondered Luis. He sat back, chewing thoughtfully on a mouthful of sundae. "Maybe you missed him."

"Twenty-four times?" Alberta shook her head firmly. "Impossible!"

"Guys, aren't you forgetting something?" Prescott said, his eyes flitting back and forth between his two friends. "Professor von Offel is a ghost!"

"Of course!" Luis tapped the palm of his hand lightly against his head. *"That's* why he doesn't show up on film."

Alberta continued to stare gloomily at the photos. "That would explain why Professor von Offel wouldn't let me take his picture," she said slowly. "He must know he doesn't show up on film. Otherwise, I'm sure he would have been happy to help me. He's probably honored that I chose his family for my science fair project."

"Honored? Happy?" Luis raised a dubious eyebrow as he scarfed down the rest of his sundae. "I wouldn't use those words to describe any von Offel. Try 'low-down' and 'unscrupulous.' I bet anything that Professor von Offel has some sneaky tricks up his sleeve to help Atom win the talking contest."

"Oh, my gosh," said Prescott. "What if he uses some special ghost powers to help Atom? Gary won't stand a chance!"

"We have to tell Mr. Flask," said Luis. He jumped to his feet, but Alberta grabbed his arm.

"Wait a minute. Mr. Flask is a scientist, remember?" she said. "We've tried to tell him about the professor before, but he won't believe us. We're going to need cold, hard proof to convince him."

"We have the pictures you took!" Prescott grabbed a handful of photos and held them up.

Alberta shrugged. "Some photos of an empty window?" she said. "It's not as if we can prove the professor was sitting there."

"You're right," said Luis, frowning. "Mr. Flask has already made a big deal of telling us not to make accusations without concrete proof. We're going to have to come up with something better than this."

"But how?" wailed Prescott.

"We're scientists, too," said Alberta, drumming her fingertips against the tabletop. "We'll think of something."

CHAPTER 9

May the Best Parrot Win

"**S**low down!" Atom squawked as the professor walked toward Einstein Elementary on Wednesday morning. He lurched unsteadily on the professor's shoulder, trying to keep his ear close to the headphones that were looped around his master's neck. "How do you expect me to listen to my CD when you're moving faster than the space shuttle?"

"What an ingenious device," Professor von Offel murmured, holding the portable CD player that was attached to the headphones. "Transmitting sound waves from a disc no larger than the palm of my —"

He broke off in midsentence, angling a glance at his parrot. "Space shuttle?" he inquired.

Atom shook his head. "After your time, Johannes. I'll explain when I'm done memorizing the Declaration of Independence."

The parrot pressed his ear close to the earphones and began to speak. "'There comes a time in the lives of all good men . . . '"

The professor, still staring at the CD player, didn't bother to listen. "What a pity a von Offel wasn't alive to profit from this creation," he mumbled.

"You mean to *steal* it," said Atom, lifting his head momentarily from the headphones.

"Shhh! Flask is coming out of his house," the professor hissed.

He pulled the headphones away from Atom's ears just as Mr. Flask strode down his front walk. The science teacher held Gary's cage in one hand and a stack of index cards in the other.

"Peter Piper picked a peck of pickled peppers," prompted Mr. Flask.

"Ack!" squawked Gary. "Peter Piper picked a peck of pickled peppers. Ack!"

"Is *that* the best that birdbrain can do?" whispered Atom.

The professor silenced his parrot with a glare. "Keep your beak shut, and leave the talking to *me*, for once."

"Ah, Professor! Good morning," Mr. Flask greeted his neighbor as he stepped onto the sidewalk. "It certainly is a beautiful day. Shall we walk to school together?"

"Ah, Professor! *Ack!* Good morning!" squawked Gary. He went on to repeat Mr. Flask's greeting, word for word.

"Excellent work, Gary!" Mr. Flask rewarded

the parrot with a handful of sunflower seeds from his lab coat pocket. "As you can see, Professor, Gary is just about ready for tomorrow's talking contest. How is Atom's training progressing?"

Atom opened his beak. But before he could say a word, the professor pinched his beak between his thumb and forefinger.

"I prefer to let Atom's talents speak for themselves at tomorrow's contest," he said to Mr. Flask. "But —"

"Yes?" Mr. Flask asked, moving alongside the professor toward Main Street.

Professor von Offel lifted one side of his mouth in a lopsided smile. "You do realize that if Gary fails to win the competition, I will be forced to write an unsatisfactory preliminary report about you to the Millennium Foundation."

Mr. Flask blinked in surprise. "What does the contest have to do with my winning the Vanguard Teacher Award?" he asked.

"The contest, which *you* proposed, is a test of your theory that Gary possesses a superior intelligence, is it not?" asked the professor.

"That's right," said Mr. Flask.

Professor von Offel aimed his bony index finger at Gary. "Well, then, if your parrot loses, your theory of Gary's superior intelligence would be proven wrong."

"Which would show faulty scientific thinking on my part," Mr. Flask finished. "I follow your reasoning, Professor von Offel."

Mr. Flask gulped. He certainly didn't want anything to threaten his chances of winning the award. But what could he do? The talking contest *had* been his idea, as the professor had pointed out.

With a sigh, the science teacher dropped his index cards into his pocket. "Luckily, I have the utmost confidence in Gary's language skills," he said. "May the best parrot win, Professor."

The professor walked stiffly forward, ignoring Mr. Flask.

Oh, well, thought Mr. Flask.

He had hoped that the talking parrot contest would help Professor von Offel loosen up and enjoy his science class more. But while the professor continued to show interest in the food science unit, his ice-cold attitude toward Mr. Flask showed no signs of thawing.

Professor von Offel didn't speak to Mr. Flask again until they reached the sixth grade science lab.

"Well! Here we are," Mr. Flask announced. He stepped into the lab — then stumbled as his sneaker caught on something.

"What —?" Professor von Offel glowered, stopping just inside the door. "What is this — this *substance* covering the floor?" he asked.

"It's plastic sheeting," Mr. Flask realized. He stepped farther into the lab, looking curiously around. "And it appears to be *everywhere*."

Plastic drop cloths completely covered the floor of the lab as well as all four walls. Even the desks and chairs were carefully wrapped. At the front of the room, Mr. Klumpp stretched a final sheet of plastic over the lab table and taped it down.

"There!" he said with a satisfied nod. "Go ahead and do your worst, Mr. Flask. I've wrapped the whole place. And I'm not going to *un*wrap it until the science fair!"

Mr. Klumpp stomped across to the door, where he stood like a sentinel. He watched smugly as the students slipped and stumbled across the sheeting to their plastic-wrapped chairs and desks.

"Our desks look like the leftovers in my grandmother's refrigerator," Alberta said, looking curiously around. "She's a maniac for plastic wrap."

"I know it's a little — unusual," said Mr. Flask, picking his way toward the lab table with sticky, squeaking steps. "But I suppose plastic wrap and food *do* go together. And we've got lots of tasty food science ground to cover today. Let's get started, class."

CHAPTER 10
Edible Earth

All the sixth graders watched while Mr. Flask opened the mini refrigerator next to the lab table and pulled out what looked like a basketball covered with pie crust.

"Presto! One Edible Earth," said Mr. Flask with a flourish. "I have to say, I'm impressed with the way you all colored parts of the pie crust blue for the oceans."

"That was my idea," said Alberta. She turned in her chair and grinned in the professor's direction. "It really makes the continents stand out, don't you think, Professor?"

At the back of the room, Professor von Offel muttered to himself. He tugged his suit jacket free of the clinging plastic on his desk and chair, then cursed under his breath as Atom tripped on the wrap, knocking over his inkwell.

"I'll get that!" Mr. Klumpp stomped across the room with a handful of paper towels. Four different times his heavy work boots caught on the drop cloth. He had to yank them free of the stuff, kicking holes in the plastic each time.

"Are you sure this is a good idea?" Mr. Flask bit his lower lip, watching as the custodian swabbed madly at the puddle of ink beneath the professor's desk. "We might be better off without the plastic."

"Never!" Mr. Klumpp fumed.

Mr. Flask sighed. "Well, if you're sure."

He took a knife and cut the globe in half, then held up one side so the inside layers showed. "Who can tell me about the different layers of our Edible Earth?" he asked.

Prescott tentatively raised his hand. "Well, the outside layer is Earth's crust, right?" he said. "That's the soil and rocks of the continents and the ocean floor."

"Everyone knows that," Max said, rolling his eyes.

"Excellent, Prescott." Mr. Flask gave an approving nod, ignoring Max. Then he pointed to the black cherry gelatin that lay just beneath the pie crust. "What about this next layer?" he asked.

"I know!" Alberta's hand shot into the air. "That's the mantle. It's made of solid rock that gets hotter and hotter the deeper into the earth you go," she said. "Eventually, it gets so hot that it melts."

"That's when we get to the next layer, the outer core. It's made of molten metal," Luis added. "We used vanilla pudding for the outer core because it's mushier than gelatin."

"Big deal. All I want to know is, when do we get to eat it?" Sean tried to slip lower in his chair, but the seat of his pants kept sticking to the plastic sheeting.

"All in good time," laughed Mr. Flask. "We still haven't identified this." He pointed to the reddish-pink layer of gelatin at the center of the Edible Earth.

"Why is there raspberry gelatin in the *middle* of the earth?" Heather asked. "I mean, gelatin represents solid earth, right?"

Every male head bobbed up and down, making Alberta roll her eyes. What was it about Heather Patterson that made sixth grade boys fall over themselves to impress her?

"But if Earth gets hotter and hotter toward the center" — Heather crinkled up her nose, staring at the Edible Earth in confusion — "shouldn't the very middle be melted, like the outer core?"

"Excellent question!" Mr. Flask held up the Edible Earth and looked out over the lab with questioning eyes. "Who can answer it?"

"I can!" Alberta said, beating out Max, Luis, Prescott, and a half dozen other boys who raised their hands.

She turned to Heather. "Even though the earth gets hotter in the middle, it also gets denser. So even though the metal of the inner core is hotter than in the outer core, gravity there is so strong that it keeps the rock solid."

"That's right!" Mr. Flask nodded his agreement, then put the two halves of the Edible Earth on the lab table. "We'll get a sampling of the four layers at the end of class."

He held up a hand to silence the groans that rose from his students. "In the meantime, we'll work on today's food science experiment, the Density Stacker."

"Density Stacker?" Max repeated. "What's that?"

"Do we get to eat it?" asked Sean, licking his lips.

"Well, you *can*, but I'm not sure you'll want to," said Mr. Flask. His eyes sparkled as he walked over to a clear plastic vat that sat on the floor next to the experiment table. "We'll be putting molasses, milk, vegetable oil, water, and vinegar together in here to test how dense they are."

Mr. Klumpp's face went white as Mr. Flask arranged gallon-sized bottles of the different liquids next to the vat. "Don't tell me —" the custodian grumbled.

But the excited students all leaned forward. "So when we pour the liquids in," said Alberta, "the densest ones will sink to the bottom, while the lighter ones will float to the top."

"Absolutely. I've collected a few other items, too." Mr. Flask pointed to a cork, eraser, paper clip, and superball that lay in a small pile on the experiment table. "Once all the liquid is poured, we can add them to see how dense *they* are compared to the different liquids. Of course, I'll need some volunteers to get it all set up."

"Me! Me!" everyone cried.

Plastic squeals rose from the lab as students jumped from their chairs.

"Whoa!" Alberta stumbled and grabbed the back of her chair. "This plastic is impossible!" she said. "Every time I move, something gets stuck."

"No kidding," said Prescott. He nearly spilled a large bottle of molasses as he carried it over to the Density Stacker.

"Careful!" Mr. Klumpp jumped forward, then gave a frustrated kick as the plastic clung to his boots once more.

"Move slowly, everyone," cautioned Mr. Flask. "Just keep calm, and there won't be any accidents — I hope."

The custodian was everywhere at once. He slipped and slid on the plastic, hunching protectively over every bottle that was poured.

"How are we supposed to keep calm with

Mr. Klumpp breathing down our necks?" Prescott whispered to Luis. "He acts like it's a national emergency every time a single drop spills!"

Luis shook his head as Mr. Klumpp tripped on the plastic sheeting for the zillionth time. "Serves him right," he whispered. "It's his own fault."

Gary let out a squawk from his cage, which hung from the coatrack just behind Luis. "It's his own fault! Ack!"

"What!" The custodian whirled around — and had to grab the lab table to keep from losing his balance. His face went bright red as he faced Gary. "Why, you sassy little —"

"Awk! It's his own fault!" Atom screeched. He took off from the professor's desk and flew toward the custodian. "It's his own fault!"

Both parrots kept up the chant, drowning out every other noise in the lab.

"Stop it!" Mr. Klumpp sputtered. He shook his fist, chasing after Atom as the parrot flew overhead. "I won't put up with —"

74

At that moment, the custodian's work boot slipped on the plastic drop cloth, ripping a huge hole in it. He flew forward with flailing arms.

"Noooo!" he cried.

"Mr. Klumpp!" Mr. Flask leaped forward.

A second too late.

The custodian smashed into the Density Stacker, knocking it over with the full force of his body.

"Oh, no!" wailed Prescott. "I can't look."

Mr. Klumpp hit the floor with a splattering thud. Molasses, oil, water, vinegar, and milk rained all over the lab. The custodian slid across the slimy, sticky, oily mess, driving it through every hole in the plastic sheeting. While he scrambled to push himself up, Atom coasted calmly above.

"Awk!" he squawked one final time. "It's his own fault!"

CHAPTER 11

The Telltale Teacup

Prescott pedaled his bike as fast as he could down Main Street after dinner that night. He turned off at the town park, riding along the paths until he came to the top of a hill at the far end.

"Bingo," he said to himself.

The grassy sports fields of Einstein Elementary spread out before him at the foot of the hill. Alberta and Luis looked like small flashes of color as they streaked around the track in the distance.

Prescott coasted down to the track, reaching his friends as they finished their run.

"What's the big emergency?" he asked, jumping off his bike and letting it fall to the ground. "Don't tell me you dragged me all the way here just so I could watch you do your cooling-down exercises."

"Sorry to ruin your training to be a couch potato, Prescott," said Alberta. She bent over one knee, then the other, in a series of stretches. "But I found something important in those photos I took."

"The ones where the professor didn't show up?" Prescott sat down on the grass next to the track and twisted a piece of grass in his fingers.

Luis nodded. He finished his own stretches, then pulled the Foto Bin envelope and a magnifying glass from Alberta's sports bag.

"Check it out," he said, handing them to Prescott.

Prescott took out the stack of photos and

stared through the magnifying glass at the top one. "I still don't see the professor," he said. He looked puzzled.

"He's a ghost. He's not going to show up," said Alberta. She and Luis plunked themselves down on either side of Prescott. "But look what does show up!"

She pointed to a spot in the photograph in the middle of the professor's lighted kitchen window.

Prescott peered carefully through the magnifying glass. "The teacup!" he gasped. "It's suspended in midair! And look. It's tipped up, exactly the way it would be if someone was drinking it."

"Cold, hard proof that Professor von Offel is a ghost," said Luis, nodding. "Even a scientist like Mr. Flask will have to believe us now." Luis and Alberta grinned and exchanged high-fives.

Prescott looked up from the photograph. "Shouldn't we show this to Mr. Flask right away?" he said excitedly. "I mean, the talking contest between Atom and Gary is tomorrow, right after the science fair. If Professor von Offel is planning to use his ghost powers —"

"Then we have to do everything we can to make sure he doesn't," Alberta finished. "And that definitely means telling Mr. Flask."

They made it to their teacher's house in five minutes flat. All three sixth graders were still catching their breath when Mr. Flask opened his front door.

"Mr. Flask! We have something important to show you," said Luis. He glanced furtively in the direction of the von Offel house next door. "Can we come in?"

"Sure. What's on your minds, scientists?" Mr. Flask led them to his living room, where Gary sat in his cage on the coffee table. On the wall, Mr. Flask's high-resolution video screen — a panel no thicker than a wafer — was mounted in between framed drawings of old-fashioned inventions.

"Um, Mr. Flask? Could we talk without Gary being here?" Luis asked.

Mr. Flask looked surprised. But he picked up Gary's cage and headed for the kitchen. "I'll be right back," he said.

"Good thinking," Prescott whispered to Luis. "We don't want Gary blabbing what we say all over Einstein Elementary."

When Mr. Flask returned, Alberta was staring at one of the framed drawings on the wall. "This is so cool, Mr. Flask," she said. "That man looks like he's strapped to some kind of helicopter."

"You're exactly right, Alberta," said their teacher. "That flying machine was a remarkable concept in its day."

Prescott stepped up behind Alberta and peered at the drawing. "Helicopters aren't exactly rare," he said.

"Not today. But they didn't exist back when this drawing was made more than four hundred years ago by Leonardo da Vinci."

"The painter?" asked Prescott.

"He was also a great inventor," Mr. Flask explained. "Da Vinci made sketches for flying machines and submersibles that were hundreds of years ahead of their time. A lot of his inventions were hard for the people of his time to understand."

"Speaking of hard to understand" — Luis caught Alberta's eye and nodded at the Foto Bin envelope in her hand — "we have something to show you, Mr. Flask."

Alberta spread out the photos on Mr. Flask's coffee table. She, Prescott, and Luis all talked at once, telling Mr. Flask about the photos Alberta had taken and showing him the teacup from which the professor had been drinking.

"See?" Alberta said, pointing at the magnified teacup. "Teacups can't float in midair by themselves. Professor von Offel was holding it, but he doesn't even show up in the photograph."

"Just the teacup appears," Prescott went on. "Floating in the air right where Professor von Offel was holding it."

"That's proof that Professor von Offel is a ghost!" Luis finished. "And we think he's going to do something tricky to make sure Gary loses the talking contest tomorrow."

"We wanted to warn you ahead of time," said Alberta.

"The proof, the whole proof, and nothing but the proof," said Luis.

The lab assistants waited for Mr. Flask to agree with them. But he just sat on the sofa, gazing at the photos on the table in front of him. It seemed like forever before he finally put the magnifying glass down.

"Well?" Alberta prompted. "You see what we're talking about, don't you?"

Mr. Flask leaned back against the sofa cushions with a sigh. "I don't know why you three insist on believing in such hocus-pocus," he began.

"But we have proof!" Prescott insisted. He jumped forward, shaking the photos under his teacher's nose. "Take another look at these. It's all there — in color!"

Mr. Flask grabbed one of the photographs and pointed at the dark speck in the professor's lighted kitchen window. "That so-called 'teacup' could be nothing more than a piece of lint in the camera lens," he said. "I'm surprised at you three. Your work on our food science unit has been careful, logical, and 100 percent scientific."

Alberta drew herself up taller. "We do our best, Mr. Flask," she said proudly.

"Yet when it comes to Professor von Offel," said their teacher, "you insist on jumping to outlandish, *un*scientific conclusions like this one!"

Prescott, Alberta, and Luis just looked at one another.

"Science is about applying logical reasoning to observations," Mr. Flask went on.

"That's what we did!" wailed Prescott. "And when we tried to *logically* reason out why Professor von Offel didn't show up in the photographs, we came up with the only *logical* conclusion."

"He's a ghost!" Alberta and Luis said at the same time.

Mr. Flash shook his head firmly back and forth. "If Professor von Offel isn't in your picture, it's not because he's a ghost," he said patiently. "It's because he was never in that window to begin with."

CHAPTER 12

The von Offels: Awful or Awesome?

"So," Prescott said to Alberta and Luis the next morning, "we just give up on trying to convince Mr. Flask that the professor is a ghost?"

The three lab assistants maneuvered Alberta's huge cardboard display carefully among the parked cars and crowds of students, parents, and teachers who clogged the entrance to Einstein Elementary.

"No way," Luis said firmly. "We keep looking for evidence. And we definitely keep a close watch on Professor von Offel."

"Not that we'll have much time, with the science fair going on all day," Alberta pointed out. "Thanks for helping me bring my project to school, guys. I never could have carried this thing by myself."

"No problem," said Luis. "Our exhibit is already set up. Prescott and I did a study of the bacteria in our mouths compared to bacteria in other animals' mouths. Mr. Flask's dog, Edgar, and his orangutan, Uri, were our case studies."

"Cool!" said Alberta.

"Our findings still give me the creeps," said Prescott. "Who knew what bacteria I was carrying around? Yech!"

"Your project looks pretty cool, too," Prescott told Alberta, "even if it *is* about those von Offels. I like the scale models of the von Offels' most famous inventions. And the whole display is in the shape of Johannes von Offel's first big invention."

"The figure-eight rubber band." Alberta's face glowed as she gazed up at the double-looping display. "I can't wait until Professor von Offel sees it."

Luis flicked a finger at the words Alberta had written in bold letters at the top of her display: THE VON OFFELS: AWFUL OR AWESOME?

"Your project is pretty heavily weighted on the Awesome side, Alberta," he pointed out. "There's hardly anything on the Awful side at all!"

"I can't help it if the von Offels were the most amazing scientific minds Arcana has ever seen," said Alberta.

"Half of those awards were stolen right out from under the Flasks," Luis insisted. "Like the award for inventing a groundbreaking new tranquilizer."

"Adolphus von Offel submitted that patent. I saw the paperwork myself," Alberta said. "He won that award fair and square."

Luis rolled his eyes. "My dad told me it was Mildred Flask Tachyon who really invented that tranquilizer. But she didn't get credit for it because her carriage horses fell asleep on the way to the patent office!"

Alberta stepped carefully up the curb toward the entrance, then glared back at Luis. "So?"

"*So* . . . Adolphus von Offel used the tranquilizer on the Flasks' horses so *he* could steal the formula and get a patent first!" he said.

Alberta shrugged. "There was never any proof of that," she said.

"But there *was* a police inquiry." Prescott pointed to the Awful side of Alberta's double loop. "You even wrote about it, Alberta."

"Nothing was ever proven," Alberta said again.

"What about the patent for laughing gas that Éduard von Offel submitted?" said Luis. "Don't you think it's suspicious that Mildred Flask's son reported his own formula for laughing gas stolen? He fell into a fit of hysterical laughter right after a visit from —"

"Let me guess," Prescott put in. "Éduard von Offel?"

Luis nodded. But Alberta held her ground.

"Rumors," she said. "I've done a lot of research, and there's not one bit of scientific proof."

She frowned, trying to push through the crowd. "Why didn't we come earlier? I really want to get set up before Professor von Offel comes, so he'll be sure to see my project. Do you see him anywhere?"

Luis looked around. He winced as two girls jabbed their plaster of paris solar system into his ribs from behind. "Professor von Offel is about the only person in Arcana who *isn't* here," he said. "You'd think that old crackpot would at least show up for a science fair."

They inched their way into the gym and set up Alberta's display on the table Mr. Klumpp had assigned to her. There was still no sign of the professor.

"There's Mr. Flask!" Prescott said. He

pointed to their teacher. Even from across the gym, the three lab assistants could sense Mr. Flask's energy and enthusiasm. His lab coat was like a white blur that flitted from table to table.

"Hello, everyone!" Mr. Flask said as he came up to them. "Alberta, your display on the von Offels is shaping up to be spectacular."

He pointed to a cardboard model of a stick attached to an old-fashioned engine. "I see you've included a model of Johannes von Offel's steam-powered walking stick. You know, my great-great-great-great-great-grandfather Jedidiah invented something quite similar, but —" He shook himself, then turned to the sixth graders with a smile. "Never mind. Good work, Alberta." He turned as Dr. Kepler walked up.

"A project on the von Offels. How wonderful!" the principal exclaimed. She read the title of Alberta's display, then said, "I hope you haven't found out anything *too* awful about the professor's family."

"If you only knew," Luis muttered.

Dr. Kepler blinked. "Excuse me?"

"Luis just means that the von Offels are even more *awesome* than any of us suspected!" Alberta said quickly, jabbing Luis in the shin with her sneaker. "Who knew?"

"Yes, well —" Dr. Kepler looked distractedly around the gym. "I'm really here about something else altogether. Has anyone seen the microwave from the teachers' lounge? It's missing."

"Missing?" Mr. Flask slipped his hands into the pockets of his lab coat. "I hope one of my students didn't borrow it for the science fair."

As he and Dr. Kepler walked off, a low growl rumbled in the air.

"What's that noise?" Luis asked.

"My stomach," groaned Alberta. "I was so busy getting my project together this morning that I skipped breakfast. I'm starved!"

"Say no more." Prescott held up a hand, then headed for the gym door. "I'll get you something from the cafeteria."

"Make it something with complex carbohydrates, okay?" Alberta called after him. "Like a bagel!"

Once Prescott got away from the gym, there weren't nearly so many people around. The halls were deserted. Even the service counter at the cafeteria was empty — except for one other person.

Prescott frowned at the rumpled form in front of him. "Professor von Offel?" he asked.

It was the professor, all right. He moved down the counter at a wild pace, rolling a portable laundry cart from the gym behind him.

"Aha!" The professor pounced on the sandwich shelf like a half-starved lion. He swept every sandwich, muffin, and bagel into the laundry cart before moving on to the beverages.

Prescott's mouth dropped open. "I've heard of food cravings," he mumbled, "but this is ridiculous!"

The professor emptied the shelves of milk, juice, soda, and a dozen containers of yogurt. The pile of food in the laundry cart grew higher and higher, until items began toppling over the side.

Even then, the professor didn't stop.

"Atom, come here!" Professor von Offel commanded.

Prescott had been so focused on the heaping mountain of food in the laundry cart, he hadn't even noticed the professor's parrot. Now he saw that Atom hovered just behind Professor von Offel.

A huge shopping bag hung from the parrot's beak. Atom flapped his wings madly, barely keeping aloft, while the professor tossed apples, pears, oranges, and grapefruits into the bag.

"No more! No more!" Atom mumbled. The heavy plastic handles weighed down his beak so that his words came out completely garbled. "Wha' do 'ou fink I am, a cargo 'elicopter?"

"This can't be real," Prescott mumbled. "No way."

He closed his eyes for a moment. But when he opened them again, it was all still there: the professor, the laundry cart of food, and Atom hovering behind with the shopping bag.

"There! That ought to do the trick," said the professor. He tossed a final grapefruit into Atom's shopping bag, then wheeled the laundry cart right past Mrs. Hagstrom, the gray-haired woman who sat behind the cash register.

"Professor?" Mrs. Hagstrom called out. "You haven't paid!"

Professor von Offel didn't even turn in her direction. Moving at a fast clip, he wheeled the cart through the cafeteria toward the hall. Atom struggled along behind, with the shopping bag hanging from his beak.

Prescott stared wide-eyed at what was left behind on the food service line.

"Nothing," he murmured, not quite believing it. "He took every last scrap of food in the whole cafeteria!"

CHAPTER 13

A Whale of
a Food Craving

The professor banged the cafeteria door open with his rolling cart. He pushed the cart quickly down the hall, chuckling to himself all the while.

"Keep up, Atom!" he said over his shoulder. "The moment of my triumph is near!"

"Easy for 'ou to 'ay!" the parrot squawked, struggling to keep the heavy bag aloft.

The moment he followed the professor into the sixth-grade science lab, Atom spat out the plastic handles. The shopping bag fell to the floor with a resounding thud.

"Phew!" Atom collapsed onto one of the desktops, gasping for breath. "Would you mind telling me why we're loaded down like this? I think my beak is broken!"

"Come, come, Atom." The professor dropped to his knees to collect the apples, oranges, and pears that rolled from the bag. "Surely you must have figured out my plan by now."

Atom opened and closed his beak a few times before pushing himself upright with his wings. "Let me guess," he said. "You need a stockpile of food because you've decided to hibernate through the winter?"

"Bah!" The professor waved away the suggestion. "How did an unimaginative piece of poultry like you ever become my closest aide and confidant?"

"At least I'm loyal," Atom countered. "I don't see anyone else crowding around to pull you out of the crazy messes you get yourself into. Like when you accidentally locked yourself inside your steam-powered energy booster? You had hot air coming out of your ears for weeks after I rescued you!"

"As I recall, my hearing improved greatly after the incident," the professor said, smiling to himself. "Though my theory that my body would gain substance did not, alas, prove to be true."

Atom hopped onto the laundry cart and picked his way across the mountain of food. "So what's it going to be this time?" he asked.

"Flask has finally done it! Like all Flasks before him, he has provided the seed for a von Offel's success." A maniacal gleam sparkled in the professor's eyes as he pulled a rolled-up sheet of paper from his jacket pocket. "I have been carefully observing Flask's food science experiments. And I have determined that the secret to returning fully to my body lies in absorbing a superblast of nutrition!"

"This stuff?" Atom pecked doubtfully at a

package of cinnamon buns. "Trust me, Johannes. The only thing you'll get from eating all this is a superblast of stomachache!"

"That might be true — *if* I leave the food in its present form," said the professor. "But I plan to transform it into a highly concentrated, superfortified nutritional nugget that will make me whole again!"

Atom covered his head with his wings. "Oh, brother," he mumbled into his feathers. "Here we go again."

"Look!" said the professor, undaunted.

He unrolled the paper scroll and jabbed a bony finger at the ink-splattered sketches, formulas, and chemical reactions scrawled across it.

"This time I've hit on a plan that is genius. Pure genius!" he crowed. "You'll see, Atom. Before the end of the day, I shall become fully human once more."

CHAPTER 14

Where's My Bagel?

Alberta and Luis were just putting the finishing touches on Alberta's display when Prescott came running up.

"You guys aren't going to believe this," Prescott said.

Alberta frowned at Prescott's empty hands. "Where's my bagel? You forgot it?" she asked.

"There weren't any bagels. There wasn't any food at all!" said Prescott. "Professor von Offel stole it all."

"He *stole* it?" Luis crossed his arms over his chest and stared at Prescott. "All the food in the whole cafeteria?"

"Yes!" Prescott's head bobbed wildly up and down. "He had a laundry cart filled with the stuff. And you should have seen Atom. He was *talking*!" Prescott said, his mouth moving a mile a minute. "I mean, he was kind of hard to understand, what with that shopping bag hanging from his beak and all. But he was definitely talking. Not like a parrot — like a *person*!"

"Prescott! You're babbling," said Alberta. She grabbed him by the shoulders and shook him. "Slow down. Now, take it from the top, okay?"

Prescott took a few deep breaths and started over. Alberta and Luis listened, getting more worried with every word they heard.

"Professor von Offel is definitely up to something," Luis said when Prescott was finished. He pointed at Alberta's display. "And whatever it is, I bet it belongs on the Awful side of your project, Alberta."

"You don't know that for sure," Alberta insisted. "Maybe the professor is just really hungry. Or maybe he's working on some really important scientific experiment."

"Or maybe he's up to some no-good ghost business," Luis shot back. "The talking contest between Atom and Gary is this afternoon after the science fair, remember? We've got to make sure the professor doesn't do something sneaky!"

Prescott shivered. "It's not like we can go to Mr. Flask. He's already fed up with our theory about the professor being a ghost," he said.

Alberta glanced across the gym, where Mr. Flask was bent over a display of a radio-controlled model dinosaur. "Besides, we still don't have any proof that the professor is a ghost *or* that he's up to something sneaky."

"Then we'll have to find out on our own what he's doing with all that food. It's up to us to stop him from using his ghost powers against Mr. Flask." Luis strode toward the hall, then waited at the gym door for Alberta and Prescott to catch up. "Come on. Let's go see if the professor is in the science lab."

Professor von Offel was indeed in the sixth grade lab, standing on a ladder next to an enormous copper vat. The vat was taller than the professor and as big around as a garbage can. It was crammed with a mishmash of foods that blended into a brownish ooze.

"Eeeew!" screeched Atom, coasting above the huge container. "That stuff looks about as appetizing as the wildebeest brain you've got pickled in formaldehyde at home."

"This is science, Atom! Not some sickening sentimental display of heart-shaped cookies," said Professor von Offel. He grabbed several cans of soda, the last items left in the laundry cart, and popped their lids open. "The hopper is almost fully loaded. In an instant we can proceed with the experiment!"

With a chortling laugh, he emptied the liquids into the copper vat. The soda splashed over the fruit, vegetables, and candy bars that bobbed on top of the brown ooze.

"You're *sure* you want to eat that stuff?" Atom squawked.

He dodged the empty cans as the professor tossed them aside. Flapping his wings, the parrot landed among the dozens of empty soft drink cans, juice boxes, and cellophane wrappers that lay scattered on the floor.

"Don't you ever listen? I'll eat it *after* it has been transformed by my super-high-density food enhancer," said the professor.

He gestured to the maze of tubes and wires that twisted out of the copper vat. They wound around the lab table, where they were attached to the back of a small microwave oven. "Once the machine has been activated, the food will pass through the transformation chambers," he said, "which will distill the material into a —"

"I know, I know. Into a highly concentrated

superfortified nutrition nugget," Atom squawked. "I just hope no one comes looking for the microwave you stole from the teachers' lounge."

"This microwave device is a vital part of my most brilliant scientific endeavor yet! That's where the nutritional nugget will appear in its final form," said the professor. "Besides, I did the principal a favor by removing the teachers' microwave. A teacher's job is to teach! A system that allows educators to lounge about warming up tepid coffee should be forbidden."

Atom hopped on top of the microwave. "Oh, sure. But it's okay for you to hijack school equipment and hide out in here doing crazy experiments when you should be evaluating Mr. Flask for the Vanguard Teacher Award?"

"Absolutely," said the professor without hesitation.

Still poised at the top of the ladder, he nodded toward the microwave. "I've set the timer to six hours. According to my calculations, that is the precise time needed to reduce the contents of the hopper," he said. "Throw the switch, Atom!"

Atom hopped over to a control panel built into the base of the enormous copper hopper. It had lights, dials, and a red metal lever. Atom hopped onto the lever and flapped his wings to push the switch to the ON position.

"Here goes!" he screeched.

The machine immediately jumped to life, shaking and buzzing intensely. Lights flashed, and whistles sounded. The dials on the control panel whirled out of control. A sucking sound like an out-of-control vacuum cleaner came from the top of the vat.

"Excellent! The contents are already being pulled into the transformation chambers," Professor von Offel announced, rubbing his hands together gleefully.

"This thing is shaking like crazy!" Atom hopped away from the control panel and shielded his head with his wings. "There's no way it can go on for six hours. It'll blow sky-high!"

Professor von Offel glanced at the timer on the microwave oven. "Astonishing!" he exclaimed. "The timer is counting down so fast that the numbers are just a blur."

Ding!

The machine went perfectly still.

Atom uncovered his head and looked up in surprise. "It's done? Already?" he asked.

He flew to the experiment table and used his beak to open the microwave's door. A cloud of smoke burst forth. Atom coughed, waving the smoke away with his wings until he could finally see the contents of the microwave.

"Well?" asked the professor, climbing down from the ladder.

"A cupcake? *That's* the best this contraption can do?" squawked Atom.

"Come now. Just because it's spectacularly brilliant science doesn't mean it can't be fun to eat," the professor scolded. He held out his hand. "Give it here."

Atom shrugged. "Whatever," he said. He hopped into the microwave and tried to grab the cupcake with his beak.

"This thing is heavier than it looks," he squawked. He tried again to get his beak around the cupcake, then reached out a foot with its talons extended. "I can't seem to get a hold on — hey!"

All of a sudden, the cupcake rolled away from him. It bounced out of the microwave, skittered across the top of the lab table, and fell to the floor.

Boing!

The cupcake ricocheted off the floor and shot up to the ceiling.

"Wow!" screeched Atom. He took off and flew through the science lab. His eyes moved up and down, up and down, following the cupcake as it bounced between floor and ceiling, over and over again. "That's some cupcake!"

"Fascinating," said Professor von Offel, watching the bouncing cupcake through his monocle. "It's so superconcentrated that it defies the laws of physics."

As Atom flew, he moved his head in all directions, trying to follow the cupcake's wild path. "Don't look now, but I think it's speeding up," he said. "It's going so fast, I'm starting to get dizz —"

WHAM!

The cupcake slammed into the back of Atom's head.

"Ooooh," he groaned.

Atom's eyes went blank. He fell to the floor like a stone.

CHAPTER 15

Catch That Cupcake!

" **A** tom, are you all right?" Professor von Offel cried.

He ran over and picked up the stunned parrot. "Still breathing," he murmured. Atom didn't move.

Crash!

The cupcake smashed into beakers on the lab table, then ricocheted into the storage cabinet, denting the door.

"That precious supercharged energy should be going into my body, not destroying the science lab!" The professor dived after the cupcake, but he couldn't catch up with it. The cupcake moved at lightning speed, bouncing off all surfaces in the science lab. Within seconds, every test tube and beaker was smashed to bits.

"Oh, no! Not the animals —"

Dropping Atom on the experiment table, the professor leaped in front of the cages. He tried to intercept the speeding cupcake, but —

Smash!

The flying cupcake bounced into a half dozen cages. Garter snakes, field mice, turtles, and an iguana slithered, skittered, and crawled across the floor.

"Professor von Offel?" a voice came from across the lab.

The professor picked himself up from the floor to find Alberta, Prescott, and Luis standing just inside the door.

"I don't see any stolen food," Luis whispered to Prescott. "But the lab is a wreck! What happened to —"

"Don't just stand there!" cried Professor von Offel, brushing shattered glass and three field mice from his suit. "Help me catch that cupcake!"

The three lab assistants looked curiously around. "Cupcake?" said Alberta. "I don't see any —"

Bonk!

The cupcake bounced off her head, hit the top of the doorway, and hurtled down the hall.

"Ouch!" cried Alberta. She rubbed her head and stared down the hallway. "Oh, my gosh. It *is* a cupcake!"

"It's bouncing around like an atomic-powered superball!" said Prescott.

He jumped back as the professor barreled past him, bits of glass still falling from his rumpled suit. "Just stop it!" the professor commanded.

Luis frowned while the professor ran after the careening cupcake, which dented lockers and smashed into the fluorescent lights.

"Why should we help him?" Luis said under his breath. "It's obvious that he just totally wrecked Mr. Flask's lab, and —"

"Guys?" Prescott interrupted. "Don't look now, but that cupcake is going faster every second. And it's headed straight for —"

"The science fair!" wailed Alberta. "And my display is right next to the door!"

She sprinted down the hall, with Luis and Prescott right behind her. They passed Professor von Offel in a matter of seconds. Leaving him wheezing in the hallway, they raced around the corner toward the gym.

"It's moving so fast, all I see is a blur!" Prescott cried.

"And it's going right into the gym. We're too late!" gasped Luis.

The cupcake rocketed through the gym door just in front of them. Alberta raced in after it and cupped her hands around her mouth.

"Get down!" she bellowed.

Crash!

Bang!

Smash!

The cupcake ricocheted around the room, wrecking everything in its path.

"No!" Prescott threw up his arms to avoid the shower of plaster bits that rained down from the plaster of paris solar system after the cupcake smashed through it. Across the gym, the aluminum head was knocked off a radio-controlled robot and smashed into one of the gym windows.

Parents, students, and teachers gaped with open mouths. Some dropped to the floor and cowered there, arms over their heads. Others ran for the door. Shrieks echoed through the air as the cupcake hit unsuspecting bystanders in its whizzing path around the gym. Cardboard, metal, paper, glass, and plastic flew through the air in every direction.

"My project!" Alberta ran toward her display. "Help me get it out of the wa —"

Smash!

The cupcake tore a baseball-sized hole right through the middle of the Awesome loop of the cardboard display.

"No!" Alberta cried. She dived forward as the rest of the display toppled off the table. "Stop that cupcake!"

Luis and Prescott raced after the speeding blur. But the cupcake was way ahead of them. It ricocheted off the basketball hoop at the far end of the gym, then shot back toward the lab assistants.

"Ouch!" yelled Prescott as the cupcake bounced off his shoulder.

By the time he reached up to rub the sore spot, the supersonic cupcake had already catapulted clear across the room. With a faint whizzing noise, it shot through the hole in the window that had been made by the robot's head.

"Finally!" Luis raced over to the window, watching the cupcake grow smaller and smaller as it bounced into the distance. Half a second later, it bounded over the treetops and was gone from sight.

An eerie quiet filled the gym. As Prescott, Alberta, and Luis looked around, incoherent mumblings rose from the wrecked displays, dioramas, and experiments. Little by little, people crawled out from underneath the wreckage and shook themselves off.

"What — *was* that?" Dr. Kepler asked, brushing a stray circuit board and some wires from the front of her suit.

"Um, maybe Professor von Offel can explain," said Prescott.

He nodded toward the doorway, where Professor von Offel stood, hunched over and wheezing.

"Professor?" Dr. Kepler prompted.

The professor glanced uneasily around at the wreckage in the gym. "Well, to be sure — er, what I mean to say is —"

Just then, Mr. Klumpp walked into the gym, shaking his head and talking to himself.

"It doesn't make any sense," mumbled the custodian. "Somebody just ate all the food in the cafeteria —"

He stopped short. As he looked around the gym, all the color drained from his face.

"Noooooo!" Mr. Klumpp gasped, sucking nearly all of the air out of the room. "What happened to the science fair?"

CHAPTER 16

The Talking Parrot Contest

"Poor Mr. Klumpp," Prescott said to Alberta and Luis an hour later. "It'll take days to clean up this mess."

The three lab assistants hovered near the door, watching the custodian sweep shattered glass and bits of cardboard, paper, and clay into mounds on the gym floor. Students and parents, still dazed, began collecting what was left of the damaged science projects.

"I'm glad Dr. Kepler rescheduled the science

fair for next week," said Alberta. She held up her cardboard display, staring through the ragged opening the cupcake had ripped through it. "I'll definitely need extra time to patch this hole. Not to mention that my models of Johannes von Offel's steam-powered walking stick and artificial thunderbolt machine were totaled when the display fell."

"You'd better add something new to your project, too," said Luis. "Any von Offel who can cause *this*" — he waved his hand around at the wreckage in the gym — "definitely deserves a write-up on the Awful side of the display."

"What's Alberta supposed to write?" asked Prescott. "That Professor von Offel single-handedly wrecked the science fair with a supersonic *cupcake*? Do you know how off the wall that sounds?"

Alberta frowned. "Mr. Flask would never believe it, and the proof is probably halfway to Mars by now," she said. She shook her head in awe. "Still, to make a cupcake with that kind of power — it's totally ingenious! Do you think we could get Professor von Offel to tell us what kind of experiment he was working on?"

"Oh, please." Luis shook his head in disgust. "Professor von Offel isn't exactly going out of his way to explain things. Look at him! He's totally ignoring Dr. Kepler and Mr. Flask."

The three lab assistants picked their way around a smashed papier-mâché model of a water molecule to where the professor, Mr. Flask, and Dr. Kepler stood.

"I simply don't understand what could have caused this kind of damage," the principal said as she surveyed the debris.

Next to her, Mr. Klumpp clamped his fingers so tightly around his broom that his knuckles were white. "Total destruction," he mumbled. "And you can bet Mr. Flask is at the root of it! He always is."

"I'm afraid I'm just as confused about what

happened as you are, Mr. Klumpp," Mr. Flask said. He placed a comforting hand on the custodian's shoulder, but Mr. Klumpp shook it off.

"That's what you said after that tornado nearly ripped apart the entire school!" huffed the custodian. "Who *else* could be responsible?"

Dr. Kepler frowned thoughtfully as Mr. Klumpp stormed to the other side of the gym with his broom. "I thought I heard Alberta say something about a — cupcake," said the principal.

"Impossible." Mr. Flask shook his head. "Still, Prescott seemed to think *you* might know something about it, Professor."

Professor von Offel paid no attention to them. He just stood there staring longingly at the gaping hole in the gym window. "Gone," he murmured. "What a pity."

"Does that mean you *do* know what caused all this damage, Professor?" Dr. Kepler asked.

Professor von Offel blinked in surprise. Finally, his eyes focused on Dr. Kepler and Mr. Flask. "I know no such thing," he snapped.

"Yes, you do," Luis said firmly as he, Prescott, and Alberta reached the professor. "We saw you in the science lab with the bouncing cupcake. You told us to catch it, re-member?"

Professor von Offel's eyes flashed with irri-tation. "Mr. Flask, once again I am forced to comment on your students' lack of scientific reasoning."

Mr. Flask looked back and forth between the professor, Alberta, Luis, and Prescott. Facing his prize students, he said slowly, "We're all perplexed by what happened here. But that doesn't mean it's okay to jump to conclusions. A good scientist doesn't let irrational ideas overtake logical thought."

Alberta's face fell. "But —"

Mr. Flask shook his head. "Now, let's leave Mr. Klumpp to his work. Professor, shall we go ahead with our talking parrot contest?"

All three lab assistants gasped.

"No!" Prescott jumped forward as Mr. Flask picked up Gary's cloth-covered cage from one of the tables. "I don't think you want to do that, Mr. Flask."

"Sure I do," Mr. Flask said. "A good-spirited contest will be just the antidote we need after this morning's catastrophe. We can't hold the contest in here, of course. But there's no reason we can't use another room. Say, the cafeteria?"

Luis bit his lip. "You don't understand, Mr. Flask," he said. "Atom is — he's not an ordinary parrot."

"Where *is* Atom?" Dr. Kepler asked, nodding at the spot on Professor von Offel's shoulder where Atom usually perched.

"Wasn't he in the science lab?" Alberta whispered to Prescott and Luis. "I mean, there was a lot going on. But I kind of remember seeing him lying on the lab table."

"Atom is, er, resting in the science lab," said the professor.

"Excellent!" Mr. Flask exclaimed. "Then he

and Gary will both be in top form for the competition. Dr. Kepler has already agreed to serve as judge." He turned to Alberta, Luis, and Prescott with a wide smile. "You three spread the word to the rest of the class, and we'll all meet in the cafeteria in 15 minutes."

The three lab assistants started to object, but Mr. Flask had already moved toward the hall. The professor, right behind him, headed toward the sixth grade science lab.

"Now what?" Prescott moaned.

Luis shrugged. "The contest goes on," he said. "But at least we'll be right there watching. Professor von Offel won't get away with any funny business if *I* can help it!"

Fifteen minutes later, the entire sixth grade science class gathered around Mr. Flask, Professor von Offel, and Dr. Kepler in the cafeteria.

"What's the matter with Atom?" Max asked. "He looks kind of dazed."

Atom, perched on the professor's shoulder, stared straight ahead with blank, glassy eyes.

His feathered body swayed slightly, as if he were having a hard time keeping his balance.

"Quiet, everyone," Dr. Kepler instructed. "I don't want any coaching." She looked back and forth between Mr. Flask and the professor, who faced each other with their parrots on their shoulders. "Are you ready?" she asked.

"Ack! Are you ready?" squawked Gary from Mr. Flask's shoulder.

All of the sixth graders burst out laughing.

"I'll take that as a yes," said Dr. Kepler. "Professor, how about you and Atom?"

Professor von Offel frowned. He tapped Atom gently on the beak, but Atom didn't move or speak. "Let's just get on with it," grumbled the professor.

"All right, then." Dr. Kepler held up a pile of index cards and read from the top card. "She sells seashells by the seashore," she said, reading from the top card.

"Ack! She sells seashells by the seashore. Ack!" Gary squawked right away.

All eyes turned to Atom. The parrot stared blankly ahead without opening his beak.

"Do you think this is some kind of trick?" Prescott whispered. "I mean, Atom can sing Italian opera! A simple tongue twister like that should be a piece of cake."

"Shhh!" warned Dr. Kepler.

She flipped to the next card. "'O-oh, say can you see,'" she sang, "'by the dawn's early light . . .'"

Again, Gary repeated the words without making a single mistake. Atom failed to utter a word.

"I don't believe this," Alberta whispered. "Maybe Gary has a chance after all."

Dr. Kepler worked her way through the whole stack of index cards. She read words, phrases, and even an entire passage from the Declaration of Independence. Each time, Gary automatically squawked back every syllable, while Atom remained silent.

"Well!" Dr. Kepler looked up with a grin after she had read the last phrase. "I don't think there's any doubt about who the winner is."

"Gary!" Alberta crowed. "Congratulations, Mr. Flask!"

"Thank you. Thank you," said Mr. Flask as everyone clapped and cheered. He held up a finger, and Gary hopped onto it. "Take a bow, Gary."

"Take a bow, Gary!" mimicked Gary. "Ack!"

Mr. Flask turned to the professor and offered his hand. "No hard feelings, I hope?" he said.

"Fat chance," whispered Prescott. "Professor von Offel looks like he wants to wring Gary's neck!"

The professor glared at Mr. Flask and Gary. "Hmmph!" huffed the professor. He strode stiffly from the room, leaving Mr. Flask's hand hanging in midair.

As soon as they were alone in the hall, the professor grabbed Atom and shook him. "Pull yourself together, you shell-shocked squab!"

"*Ooooooh,*" the parrot groaned. He blinked several times, shaking himself.

"*Now* you come to your senses, *after* you've made a complete fool of me." The professor gazed at Atom with concerned eyes that flashed in and out of focus. "You *are* all right, aren't you?"

"Oh, my aching head!" Atom fluffed out his wings, trying to massage his temples. "Did anyone get the license number of the truck that hit me?"

Welcome to the World of
MAD SCIENCE!

The Mad Science Group has been providing live, interactive, exciting science experiences for children throughout the world for more than 12 years. Our goal is to provide children with fun, entertaining, and exciting activities that instill a clearer understanding of what science is really about and how it affects the world around them. Founded in Montreal, Canada, we currently have 125 locations throughout the world.

Our commitment to science education is demonstrated throughout this imaginative series that mixes hilarious fiction with factual information to show how science plays an important role in our daily lives.

To discover more about Mad Science and how to bring our interactive science experience to your home or school, check out our website:
http://www.madscience.org

We spark the imagination and curiosity of children everywhere!